Written by
Ryan Riegg

Art by
Tatiana Jiménez

Many know the story
of Athena

Goddess of Wisdom

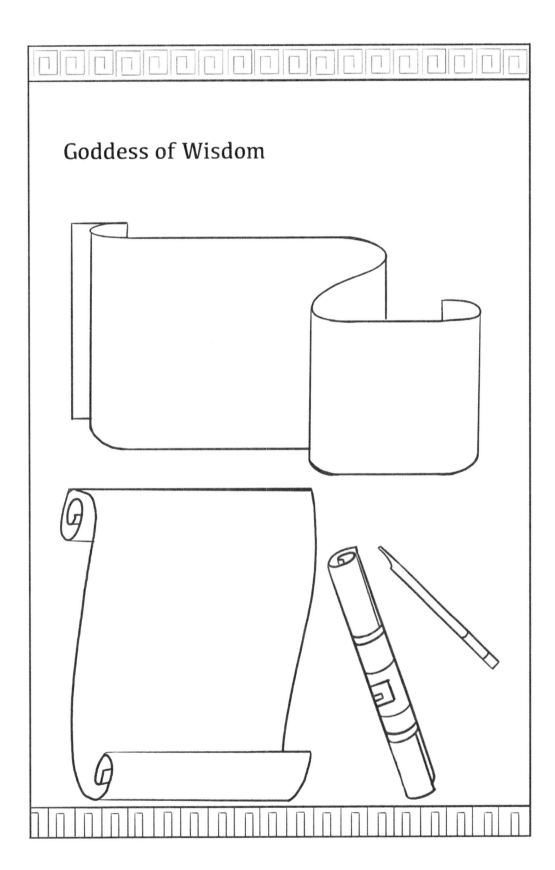

Protector of Athens

Daughter of Zeus

Athena, who saved Hercules

And Perseus

And Odysseus

And Jason

Athena, who gifted the
Olive Tree to humanity

And created weaving

And sp|ders

But few know the story of the owls who raised her.

And the wisdom
they gave her

And she gave them

Only a few know the truth

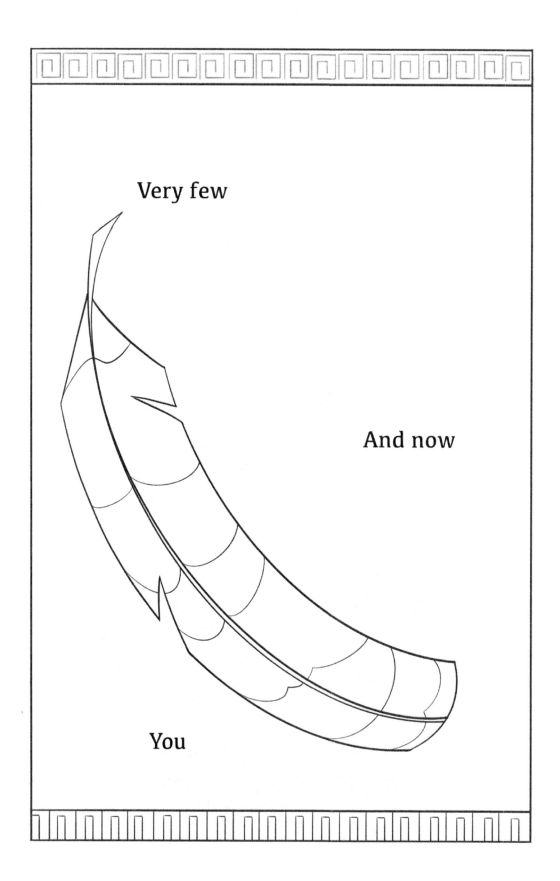

ATHENA'S OWLS

A CALL TO OLYMPUS

* "μεταμορφώνω" means transform in Greek

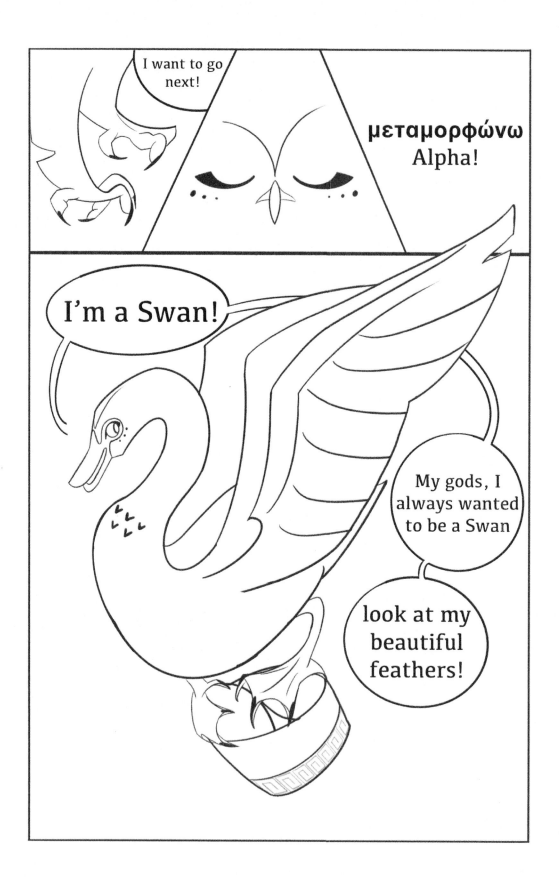

The Athena's Owls series will continue in Book II to be released later this year.

If you like the story of Athena's Owls, please feel free to collect other versions of this comic, which will be released periodically.

More information about the book series can be found at glaukopisdesign.com

This book is dedicated to my wife & daughter. Thank you for making me a better person.

Printed by Amazon Italia Logistica S.r.l.
Torrazza Piemonte (TO), Italy

56331625R00025